THE CHRISTMAS DEPARTMENT STORE

Maudie Powell-Tuck   Hoang Giang

LITTLE TIGER

LONDON

Benji's gran had always said,
"Magic happens on Christmas Eve."
  This Christmas needed some magic.
There wasn't enough money for a tree
or even a turkey, and everyone felt
a little sad.

Benji passed dazzling shops and excited shoppers.
"I wish I could buy my family spectacular presents,"
he sighed. "That might make them smile again."
But Benji's gran was right about Christmas Eve,
because when he turned to go home . . .

. . . he was bowled over by
a gigantic polar bear,
   "Sorry, sorry! I'm late
for work!"

Benji scrambled to
his feet and gasped . . .

A huge, glamorous department store had
appeared, shimmering in the frosty air.
"This way, sir," said penguin doormen, tipping their hats.

Benji blinked
at the sky-high
Christmas tree,
the snow falling
lightly from the
ceiling . . .

"It's real magic!" he marvelled.
And for the first time that Christmas,
Benji fizzed with excitement.

TOOT TOOT!
A shiny steam train puffed around the corner.
"Hop on," grinned the polar bear.
"Let's find those presents!"

They raced along a golden track, spiralling
higher and higher! Benji's head spun with
candy canes, lights and sparkly baubles.

All too soon, the train stopped.
"Here we are. The department of silly sounds," said the polar bear.

BOING! POOOWEEE!
YUMMA YUMMA TING TONG!

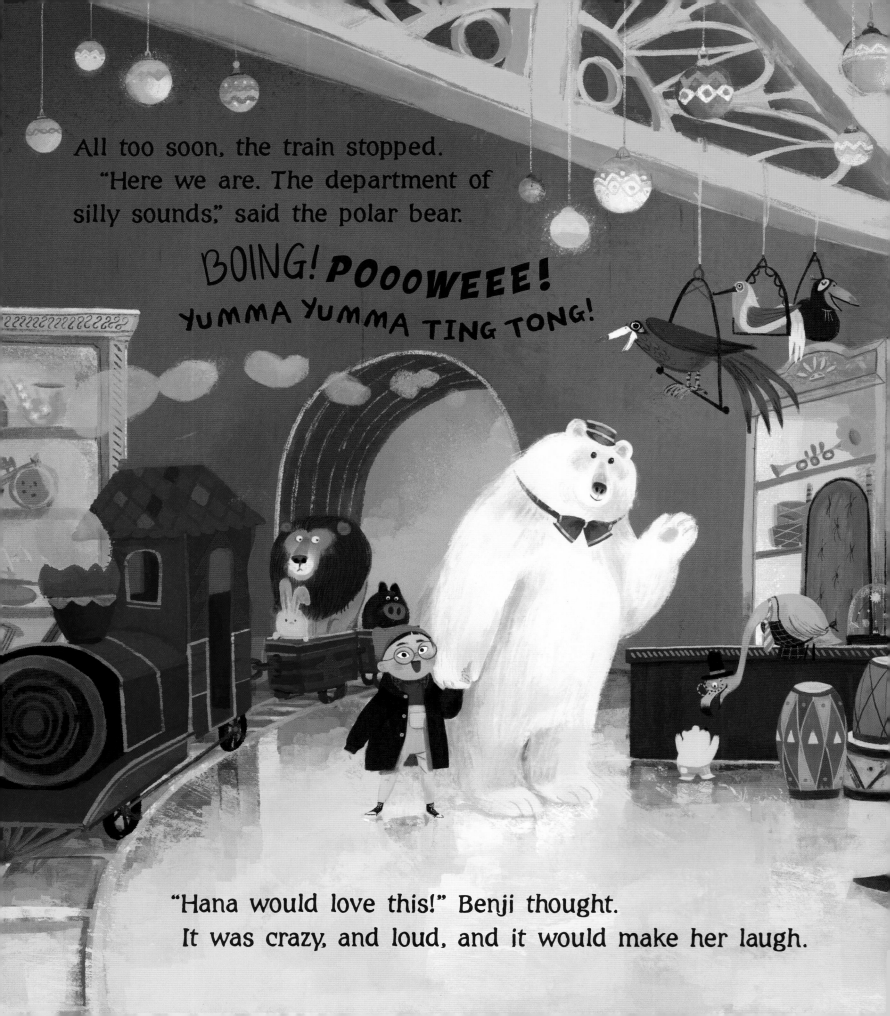

"Hana would love this!" Benji thought.
It was crazy, and loud, and it would make her laugh.

Benji blew a funny looking, twisted trumpet.
FLIPPERTY FLAARP!
"Excellent choice, sir!" enthused a flamingo. "Your sister will be thrilled."

"But I can't afford it," said Benji.
"I only have a few pounds."

"Pounds?" trilled the flamingo.
"Good Lord, we don't want your
pounds. Sing us a song instead.
The sillier the better."

The song had the flamingo in stitches.
"Goodbye!" Benji waved. "Thanks for
the trumpet!"

"Who's next on your list? Your granny?" asked the polar bear. "We have to find something VERY special for her. Next stop . . .

. . . the department of imaginary gifts!"

It was pretty empty. "There's nothing here," said Benji.

"Sir has to use his imagination,"
drawled a leopard shop assistant.

Benji closed his eyes, imagined hard,
then opened them again . . .

The department bulged with extraordinary gifts.
Genie lamps, treasure chests, bejewelled suits
of armour . . . but no perfect present for Granny.
"It's got to make her feel wonderful," said Benji.

Then he saw it: a most magnificent imaginary hat. "How much, please?" he asked.

"One exceptional story," said the leopard, packing the hat in a box. So Benji told the finest tale he could imagine and left the leopard purring with contentment.

The final gift was for his dad. It had
to be just right, Benji explained.

"Dad sometimes feels sad he can't buy us
lots of things. So when he opens my present,
I want him to feel happy. I want him to feel . . ."

"Loved?" asked the polar bear.

Benji nodded. The polar bear held his hand
and led him into a department awash with
fabulous smells like cinnamon, chocolate
and crackling fires.

"Try this," said the bear, opening a jar labelled *Excitement*. Benji sniffed and WHOOSH . . .

he was whizzing along a roller coaster.

"Let's try another", he laughed.

One sniff of a jar labelled *Summer Holidays* and he was on a beach, breathing in the salty air!

Whoosh

ahh

Woah

They smelled jar
after jar, all amazing,
but none quite right for
Dad – until the last one.
It was a small jar labelled
Joy. Benji sniffed . . .

It smelled like family movie nights
on the sofa, like walks together in the
autumn, like a cuddle from the person
you love most in the world . . .

Benji left the department store with
his bag heavy, his head full of magic.
"Goodbye, goodbye!" waved the polar bear.

Back home, Benji couldn't stop peeking at the presents.

"Someone's excited for Christmas," nudged Granny at dinner.

Hana and Benji woke
very early next morning.
   "It's Christmas!"
Hana yelled.

Granny made a special breakfast,
then they decorated Dad
with tinsel.

But when it was time to give presents, Benji paused.

He had an empty hat box, a twisted trumpet and a stupid jam jar.

These presents weren't spectacular! They were terrible!

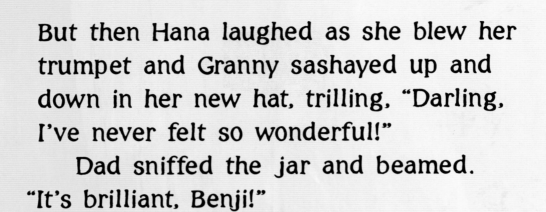

But then Hana laughed as she blew her trumpet and Granny sashayed up and down in her new hat, trilling, "Darling, I've never felt so wonderful!"

Dad sniffed the jar and beamed. "It's brilliant, Benji!"

Everyone hugged. Benji had given them
the best presents money can't buy.
They all felt happy. They all felt loved.
And Christmas was magical once again.